✓M

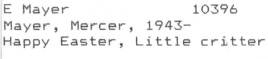

DATE DUE		APR 14 1994
MAY 20 1993	DEC 1 1993	APR 21 1994
SEP 28 1993	DEC 13 1993	MAY 24 1994
SEP 23 1993	DEC 20 1993	JUL 6 1994
	JAN 13 1994	JUL 5 1994
OCT 4 1993	JAN 20 1994	
OCT 11 1993	FEB 3 1994	OCT 24 1994
OCT 18 1993	MAR 5 1994	
OCT 25 1993	MAR 21 1994	
NOV 1 1993	MAR 28 1994	
NOV 8 1993	APR 7 1994	

Billings County Public School
Dist. No. 1
Medora, North Dakota 58645

DEMCO

HAPPY EASTER, LITTLE CRITTER®

BY MERCER MAYER

For Tanya
and Dustin

A GOLDEN BOOK • NEW YORK

Western Publishing Company, Inc., Racine, Wisconsin 53404

Library of Congress Catalog Card Number: 87-81759
ISBN: 0-307-11723-5/ISBN: 0-307-61723-8 (lib. bdg.)   MCMXC

10396

It's Easter morning.
I bet the Easter Bunny
has already come.

I'll quietly tiptoe downstairs...

and find all the Easter goodies
before anyone else wakes up.

But, as usual, my little sister
is up before me.

I got a toy egg that you can
look into, a wind-up bunny,
some candy chickens, a bunch
of chocolate eggs, and millions
of jelly beans.

The Easter Bunny gave my little sister the same things.

Dad says that's so we won't argue.

Mom says we can't eat any of it until after breakfast.

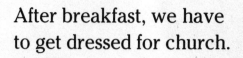

After breakfast, we have
to get dressed for church.

Dad starts the car, and we all get in.

My little sister likes to get all
dressed up, but I don't.

At church, I can't see anything because everyone is wearing funny hats.

After church, all the kids
dye Easter eggs.

I think my eggs are the best.

While the eggs dry we have a big picnic lunch.

10396

Then our parents hide the eggs in
the field. We're not supposed to peek.

Next, we all line up...

and run into the field to find the eggs.

Sometimes too many kids find the same egg.

Sometimes you walk right by an egg, and someone else finds it.

Sometimes the little kids don't find any,
so you have to help them.

But by the time we go home, everyone has
had a happy Easter.